Books by Sigmund Brouwer

Lightning on Ice Series
#1   *Rebel Glory*
#2   *All-Star Pride*
#3   *Thunderbird Spirit*
#4   *Winter Hawk Star*
#5   *Blazer Drive*
#6   *Chief Honor*

Short Cuts Series
#1   *Snowboarding to the Extreme . . . Rippin'*
#2   *Mountain Biking to the Extreme . . . Cliff Dive*
#3   *Skydiving to the Extreme . . . 'Chute Roll*
#4   *Scuba Diving to the Extreme . . . Off the Wall*

CyberQuest Series
#1   *Pharaoh's Tomb*
#2   *Knight's Honor*
#3   *Pirate's Cross*
#4   *Outlaw's Gold*
#5   *Soldier's Aim*
#6   *Galilee Man*

The Accidental Detectives Mystery Series

Winds of Light Medieval Adventures

Adult Books
Double Helix
Blood Ties

QUEST 6

GALILEE MAN

SIGMUND BROUWER

Thomas Nelson, Inc.
Nashville

To Lesley and Michelle,
great neighbors, great friends

Galilee Man
Quest 6 in the *CyberQuest* Series

Copyright © 1998
by Sigmund Brouwer

Published in Nashville, Tennessee,
by Tommy Nelson™, a division of Thomas Nelson, Inc.

Managing Editor: Laura Minchew
Project Editor: Beverly Phillips
Cover Illustration: Kevin Burke

Library of Congress Cataloging-in-Publication Data
Brouwer, Sigmund, 1959–
    Galilee man / Sigmund Brouwer.
       p. cm. — (CyberQuest; quest 6)
    Summary: Concludes the virtual reality adventures of Mok
who proves himself worthy to lead the underground movement
to restore Christianity to Old Newyork in the twenty-first century.
    ISBN 0-8499-4039-7
    [1. Science fiction. 2. Virtual reality—Fiction. 3. Christian
life—Fiction.]   I. Title.   II. Series: Brouwer, Sigmund, 1959–
CyberQuest; 6.
PZ7.B79984Gal 1997
[Fic]—dc21   97-35635
                                                              CIP
                                                              AC

Printed in the United States of America
98 99 00 01 02 OPM 9 8 7 6 5 4 3 2 1

CYBERQUEST SERIES TERMS

BODYWRAP — a sheet of cloth that serves as clothing.

THE COMMITTEE — a group of people dedicated to making the world a better place.

MAINSIDE — any part of North America other than Old Newyork.

MINI-VIDCAM — a hidden video camera.

NETPHONE — a public telephone with a computer keypad. For a minimum charge, users can send e-mail through the Internet.

OLD NEWYORK — the bombed out island of Manhattan transformed into a colony for convicts and the poorest of the poor.

TECHNOCRAT — an upper class person who can read, operate computers, and make much more money than a Welfaro.

'TRIC SHOOTER — an electric gun that fires enough voltage to stun its target.

VIDTRANS — a video transmitter.

VIDWATCH — a watch with a mini television screen.

WATERMAN — a person who sells pure water.

WELFARO — a person living in the slums in Old Newyork.

THE GREAT WATER WARS—A.D. 2031. *In the year* A.D. *2031 came the great Water Wars. The world's population had tripled during the previous thirty years. Worldwide demand for fresh, unpolluted water grew so strong that countries fought for control of water supplies. The war was longer and worse than any of the previous world wars. When it ended, there was a new world government, called the World United. The government was set up to distribute water among the world countries and to prevent any future wars. But it took its control too far.*

World United began to see itself as all important. After all, it had complete control of the world's limited water supplies. It began to make choices about who was "worthy" to receive water.

Very few people dared to object when World United denied water to criminals, the poor, and others it saw as undesirable. People were afraid of losing their own water if they spoke up.

One group, however, saw that the government's actions were wrong. These people dared to speak—Christians. They knew that only God should have control of their lives. They knew that they needed to stand up to the government for those who could not. Because of this, the government began to persecute the Christians and outlawed the Christian church. Some people gave up their beliefs to continue to receive an allotment of government water. Others refused and either joined underground churches or became hunted rebels, getting their water on the black market.

In North America, only one place was safe for the rebel Christians. The island of Old Newyork. The bombings of the great Water Wars had destroyed much of it, and the government used the entire island as a prison. The government did not care who else fled to the slums of those ancient street canyons.

Old Newyork grew in population. While most newcomers were criminals, some were these rebel Christians. Desperate for freedom, they entered this lion's den of lawlessness.

Limited water and supplies were sent from Mainside to Old Newyork, but some on Mainside said that any was too much to waste on the slums. When the issue came up at a World Senate meeting in 2049, it was decided that Old Newyork must be treated like a small country. It would have to provide something to the world in return for water and food.

When this new law went into effect, two things happened in the economy of this giant slum. First, work gangs began stripping steel from the skyscrapers. Anti-pollution laws on Mainside made it expensive to manufacture new steel. Old steel, then, was traded for food and water.

Second, when a certain Mainside business genius got caught evading taxes in 2053, he was sent to Old Newyork. There he quickly saw a new business opportunity—slave labor.

Old Newyork was run by criminals and had no laws. Who was there to stop him from forcing people to work for him?

Within a couple of years, the giant slum was filled with bosses who made men, women, and children work at almost no pay. They produced clothing on giant sewing machines and assembled cheap computer products. Even boys and girls as young as ten years old worked up to twelve hours a day.

Christians in Old Newyork, of course, fought against this. But it was a battle the Christians lost over the years. Criminals and factory bosses used ruthless violence to control the slums.

Christianity was forced to become an underground movement in the slums. Education, too, disappeared. As did any medical care.

Into this world, Mok was born.

OLD NEWYORK—A. D. 2078. "Rufus, you have no place left to run!"

From far down the long, cool tunnel, the ganglord's shout of anger echoed among the broken slabs of concrete. One wide section, the height of two men, leaned at an impossible angle, supported by the smaller pieces it had fallen upon. A shaft of sunlight streamed through a sewer grate in the street above, casting deep shadows. It was here that the man, the woman, and the baby crouched, hidden.

"Die! Die! Die!" This demented shouting came from the opposite direction in the tunnel, repeated again and again by the ganglord's warriors. The sound bounced off the jagged edges of the jumbled concrete and seemed to surround the three fugitives.

"I love you," the woman, Terza, whispered to the man.

"As I love you, my wife," Benjamin Rufus replied. He smiled sadly in the darkness of their hiding spot and tightened his arm around her shoulders.

"Can't we have more time together?" she asked. "Not even another day?"

"Shhh," he cautioned. He heard the braveness in her voice as she fought her tears. In his own sorrow, he hardly trusted himself to speak without choking on his words. He whispered, "That my illness has not taken me during my two years in the slums is a miracle. I, too, want to ask for more time. It takes effort to remember that I should instead give thanks for every extra hour God has allowed me to live with you."

The baby in Terza's arms gurgled with happiness, unaware of their danger. Benjamin held them both close, and his wife leaned her head on his shoulder. As the shouting grew closer from both sides, the man and the woman prayed in silence.

Benjamin murmured, "Remember our greatest hope, my love. For those without faith, death in this world means the end. But we have the joy given to us by Christ. Time here is short. But beyond waits an eternity of love."

"Can you be sure?" she asked as her tears began to fall.

"I have had my doubts," he said. "It is part of being human. But as death approaches, God strengthens my certainty. He *is* the creator of this universe. I do not fear Zubluk because I do not fear death."

"Just another day together," she pleaded.

"Another week. We can escape now and keep running. I cannot bear to say good-bye."

"No," Benjamin said quickly. If he allowed himself to consider it, he might take whatever time his body had left, even though he was weakened by illness. "You must leave now. Before they see you."

"I love you," she said one final time.

In answer, he found her hand and lifted it so she could feel the tears on his face.

Then Benjamin Rufus rose. He helped Terza climb the slab of concrete. She and the baby escaped through the sewer grate above.

When they were gone, he replaced the sewer grate and settled beneath the concrete slab again. And waited for the ganglord to arrive.

"I know you are here," Zubluk said into the grays and blacks of the tunnel shadows. "You were betrayed by one of your own. For only a few bottles of pure water, he told us how to find you."

"I am here," Benjamin replied from his hiding spot. He was confident that the echoes would make it difficult for them to locate him exactly.

"And your wife and child?"

"Do they matter? It is only me you want."

"I want you to pay," Zubluk said. "You have caused me too much trouble. If they are not with you, I will track them down."

Benjamin Rufus did not have to see Zubluk to know how the angry man looked. The giant always wore black leather. A fighter of many years, his battered face bore many old scars. As did his shaved head. Behind him would be his warriors. Equally fierce. Equally merciless.

"Tell me," Zubluk said. "Why? You've lived two years in the slums. Why?"

"Do you mean to distract me while your men circle around?" Rufus asked.

Zubluk laughed. "No. You're already a dead man. With you trapped like this, I don't need to play games. It is truly a question that has bothered me since you returned to the slums."

"Returned?" Rufus said. He had his own reason to keep the conversation going as long as possible. It would give his wife and baby time to get farther away. "Returned to the slums? So you know."

"Yes," Zubluk said. "I know who you are. So why did you come here from Mainside? From freedom and wealth and power and comfort? You were one of the few who ever escaped this island."

"Because where I once was blind, now I see," Rufus answered.

"Don't speak riddles with me," Zubluk snarled.

"Had you listened to the message I brought," Rufus said calmly, "you would know it is not a riddle."

"Bah!" If Zubluk thought it strange to converse with a voice coming from the darkness, nothing about his snort showed it. "A man died on a cross thousands of years ago. What does that matter to us today?"

"It is not his death that is important. But that he rose again and lives to this day. Believe, Zubluk. Fall on your knees and believe. Even after all the terror you have inflicted on the poor people here, you will be forgiven and welcomed home."

Zubluk roared with laughter. "You speak as if I were about to die. Not you."

"I know I will die," Rufus said. "My body has been failing. Even without you and your sword, very soon my spirit will leave its frail prison. I am ready. But I fear you are not."

Silence. Benjamin Rufus had spoken with such certainty that it rattled the scarred ganglord.

Rufus listened for the scuffle of leather that would tell him the warriors were closing in. He heard only the quiet drips as water condensed on and fell from the cool walls of the tunnel.

"Zubluk," he called out. "Did you not wonder why it was so easy to find me? So easy to trap me?"

More silence. Rufus touched a small plastic box attached to his belt. Had enough time passed? Were Terza and the baby safe? Had she been able to clear others from the street above?

Rufus closed his eyes in brief prayer. He opened them again, straining for the first signs of Zubluk's warriors.

Finally, he heard it. Someone kicked a pebble. Zubluk's men had found him. It was time to act.

"Zubluk," Rufus said. "Do you now under-stand? I came from Mainside with a message. It is a message the people of the slums must be freed to hear. I have weapons you do not. And I am already dying."

"Get him!" Zubluk roared.

Shadows dove toward the space beneath the large slab of concrete.

Benjamin Rufus pressed the button on the small plastic box. A button that sent a tiny electronic signal to plastic explosives wedged into crevices of the tunnel wall.

There was a flash and the horrible thunder of thousands of tons of falling concrete. A great plume of dust rose into the slums from the sewer grate.

Then, half a minute later, there was silence again. Complete silence.

CHAPTER 1

MAINSIDE—EIGHTEEN YEARS LATER (A.D. 2096). "Oxygen! Now!" The doctor snapped the order without looking over his shoulder. It was a small room, and the doctor fully expected the medtech behind him to bring the portable tank and mask within seconds.

Head still down as he examined the body on the cot, the doctor spoke in calmer tones to the man standing beside him.

"Cambridge," he said. "I don't know how long we can keep Mok alive. The monitors all show signs of major trauma. Blood pressure down. Shallow breathing. Feeble heart rate. It's as if a bullet has actually hit Mok."

The doctor shook his head and finally looked up from the patient. "I almost wish he were bleeding."

"Because . . . ?" Cambridge prompted. His face, thin and hawklike, looked tight with worry.

The medtech handed over the oxygen tank. The room contained little beyond medical equipment and Mok's body, which was attached to a life-support machine. Other lines were taped to Mok's shaved head. These ran to a nitrogen-cooled computer. Aside from the medtech, the doctor,

1

Cambridge, and of course Mok, no one else had been allowed in the room.

The doctor placed the oxygen mask on Mok's face.

As he turned dials on the tank, he said, "If he were actually bleeding, emergency surgery would stop the blood loss and stabilize him. As it is now, his body is reacting to what his mind believes, and we have no way of convincing his mind that the bullet and the wound don't exist."

Cambridge sighed. Mok was linked to a computer program designed to make virtual reality so believable it was impossible to tell it wasn't live. Once Mok believed death had struck him in cyberspace, it would scramble the nerve circuits in his brain, killing him in real time.

The doctor, short and red-headed, took another blood pressure reading. His lips tightened with concern.

"We must save him," Cambridge said in hardly more than a whisper. "Mok has just passed the final test. Without him to sway the World Senate vote, the heat bombs . . ."

Cambridge cut himself short. The doctor already knew the urgency. He didn't need the extra pressure of Cambridge telling him how thousands and thousands of slum dwellers might be fused into a molten puddle of glass and concrete and steel.

"At this point," the doctor said a few moments later, "oxygen doesn't seem to be helping. We'll need to risk emergency interference. Let's go to the back-up plan and send a doctor into cyberspace after him. Maybe virtual surgery will keep Mok from dying."

"I wish we could." Cambridge closed his eyes and pressed his hands against his face. "But we've lost Mok on the vidscreen. The comtechs are hoping we can land him at a new cybersite any second. Maybe then . . ."

Again, Cambridge found it difficult to say more. Mok had been so close to the end of the cybertests. There'd been Egypt, the test of justice. A Holy Land castle siege that tested his growing belief. A pirate ship experience that helped him learn to share his faith. The Wild West, where he was tempted with riches over truth. There he'd also learned to judge a man by his actions, not just his words—even when he knew the words to be true. And now, just after passing the test of leadership in Nazi Germany, Mok had taken a bullet from a Gestapo officer.

It had been so close. So very close. Mok had been five minutes from returning as a hero. Cambridge agonized over what had gone wrong. How had cybersecurity been breached? Mok was not supposed to have been shot. Yet Mok believed the bullet wound so real it was draining his life.

Mok's breathing grew more shallow beneath the oxygen mask. Cambridge didn't need a medical background to know it was a bad sign.

"I have no choice but to inject him with adrenaline," the doctor said. "If that doesn't work, I don't know what else to do. Or how long he'll live to let me try something else."

Cambridge put his hand on the doctor's shoulder. "I'll tell the Committee you're doing everything possible. As for us . . ."

"Yes?" the doctor asked, reaching for a hypodermic needle.

"We'll be praying," Cambridge said as he headed out of the room. "For a miracle."

CHAPTER 2

CYBERSPACE—JERUSALEM. Shouts. Wailing. Babble.

Dust. Heat. Sun. Shadows.

Slowly, one by one, Mok made sense of each new impression. It seemed an icy blackness was melting away from him, bringing him into growing light.

He became aware of hard stone pressing against his body, of rough walls around him. He smelled rotting vegetables and fruit.

With the returning sensations came another: pain.

Mok lay on his side, and as he pushed himself up, pain lanced him. Pain from his back and shoulder.

He groaned. The sensation was white heat as he forced himself to his feet. He almost fell and leaned against the wall. He felt warmth on his ribs. With shock, he realized it was blood. His blood.

Memories returned.

He'd been on a river barge. At night. In Paris. Leading a Gestapo officer holding a pistol into a trap. He'd heard a bang of exploding air. He had twisted and fallen, staring up at the city lights bouncing off the low clouds. Faces had come into view. Faces that had then faded.

And now? Where was he?

Waking up in a new time and place was no longer strange to Mok. It had happened too many times already. Ever since—what seemed like years ago—he'd been shot with a blue arc of light in the slums of Old Newyork. Mok had woken then to the hot sands of ancient Egypt. Much as he'd tried to convince himself he was dreaming, reality forced him to understand otherwise. He'd barely survived an execution order, only to have whirling darkness spin him to an ancient castle. From there, to a pirate ship, facing a hurricane and savage raids. Then to grassland prairies, where he'd learned to handle a six-shooter. And finally, to Paris during the second World War.

Indeed, Mok had learned that he could do little to control each new situation. If he waited and watched, he would discover his role. In all the previous times, though, he had never woken with his own blood soaking the clothing he wore.

Dizziness began to take Mok. Not the dizziness that signaled he would soon find himself in another time and place. But a frightening dizziness that instinct told him meant death.

He needed help.

Ahead, where the alley emptied into a street, he heard wailing and shouting. People. People who might help.

Mok staggered forward, leaving blood smears where he lurched against the stone of the wall.

A part of his mind took in the shapes of the archways and the tiled roofs. It reminded him somewhat of the streets he'd seen in Egypt, except this seemed more crowded.

The noise and babble grew louder as he neared the street. Mok found himself panting to get breath. He wanted to lie down and close his eyes, hoping for darkness to return and let him drift away.

A few more steps. People backed into the entrance of the alley, as if the crowd on the street had forced them to retreat.

Mok fell. His grunt of agony drew the attention of a large man looking over the shoulders of people in front of him.

The man turned to Mok. He bent over Mok and lifted him to his feet. If the man felt any disgust at the blood on his hands from Mok's wound, he did not show it.

"My friend," the man said, "you are in a bad way."

The man was black haired and bearded, with a square face and dark eyes. Despite his bulk, he did not appear intimidating.

"Where . . ." Mok gasped at the effort it took to speak. "Where are we?"

The man frowned. "Jerusalem. During Passover. Did thieves beat you so badly that you cannot remember?"

"It hurts," Mok said. He could not remember ever in his lifetime in the slums asking for help. Weakness meant death in Old Newyork. But Mok had little more strength than a newborn baby. And there was something gentle about this large man. "Please . . ."

Mok couldn't croak out any more words.

"I will do what I can," the man said. "Yet we cannot move until the procession passes by."

Mok leaned against the man, on his feet only because of the man's arm around his waist. The man pushed through the small knot of people. They grumbled but quieted at the sight of Mok's wound.

Only half-conscious, Mok turned his head to look at the commotion headed toward them.

It took him long moments to sort out what he saw. There were soldiers, armed with short swords. They led a man, torn and bloody. Behind the man followed a large procession. The women in the crowd wailed and cried out.

It was not the loud public grief of the women that held Mok's attention, but the bloody man guarded by soldiers. The man was bent almost in half as he dragged two large beams of wood, tied together in the shape of a cross.

CHAPTER 3

THE MARKET STREET began down a hill, so Mok clearly saw the activity below him. The soldiers whipped and prodded the man carrying the cross. It was a great load, and the man fell. One soldier kicked the man. Others spat on him.

Wailing rose from the women behind the soldiers.

Somehow, with agonizing slowness, the man got to his feet again, bowed beneath the heavy cross. He pushed up the hill. It was obvious the man was near the point of exhaustion.

Still, the soldiers jeered.

The man's slow progress finally brought him near Mok. Mok saw that the man's face streamed with blood from puncture wounds caused by the crown of thorns he wore. The man fell again. Once again, soldiers kicked him.

This time, however, the man could not get up.

The tallest soldier surveyed the crowd. Looking up the street, his eyes turned on the man supporting Mok.

"You," the soldier commanded. "What is your name?"

"I am Simon," the man said, moving slightly to

shield Mok from the soldier's sight. "Of Cyrene."

"As I thought. From the country. You have a big, strong back. You carry the cross."

"And if I don't?" Simon asked.

"No one disobeys Roman commands," came the answer. "You'll die by the sword where you stand."

Simon looked around him. The crowd was silent, awaiting his answer.

"Someone take him," Simon said, setting Mok down gently. No one moved forward.

"This young man is hurt," Simon appealed to the people around him. "He needs help."

No one moved forward except the Roman soldier. He waved a menacing sword toward the farmer. "Take the cross now or die."

"I am sorry, my friend," Simon said to Mok. His voice held no hurry. No panic or fear. "I have no choice but to leave you. If he kills me, I cannot help you later."

Simon dug into his pocket and brought out a coin. He pressed it into Mok's hand. "Take this. Perhaps someone will accept payment to bind your wounds. I will return and look for you."

Mok nodded, too tired to thank the man from Cyrene.

Simon stepped into the narrow street. He walked with his shoulders square, keeping his gaze level to those of the crowd who stared at him. He bent his back to accept the weight of the cross. His strong legs pushed upward. The wooden beams rested solidly without wavering.

The soldiers kicked the other man to his feet.

"No!" a woman wailed. She had dark hair, and tears glimmered on her face. "This man is innocent! Let him live!"

Other women cried the same cry.

The man of the cross turned to them. "Women of Jerusalem," the man said, "Don't cry for me. Cry for yourselves and for your children."

Whatever else the man said was lost to Mok, for the people around him began to press forward.

Mok tried to rise but was too weak. He fell back.

Through the legs of the people in front of him, Mok saw the procession begin to move up the hill again. Soldiers in front. The man among the soldiers. Simon behind. And the multitude of people following.

A few steps later, when the whipped and beaten man came opposite Mok, he stopped.

As if directed by an invisible hand, the people in front of Mok parted.

Mok, bleeding and exhausted from his own pain, raised his head. His eyes met the eyes of the man of the cross. A man with no significant features. A face neither ugly nor handsome. Hair neither long nor short. A build not powerful, not weak. Someone easy to overlook in a crowd. Except for his eyes.

The man's face was white from utter weariness.

His beard was matted with blood and spittle. Yet the eyes . . .

The depth of the man's eyes lifted Mok's heart, thrilled Mok with an unspeakable peace.

The man reached out with a trembling hand.

A soldier knocked the man's hand away. Yet the man reached again toward Mok.

Mok was drawn to his feet. He somehow found the strength to reach out to the man of the cross.

"You are loved," the man said to Mok, his soft voice clear in the crowd's surging noise. "I know of your burdens, your pains. Follow me to my Father, and you shall find a home. Never again will you be lonely and afraid."

One of the soldiers stepped between them. The man stood strong, just for a moment, and his finger-tips brushed against Mok's. It was the lightest touch, like the graze of dove's wing.

The crowd's noise filled the space between them. The soldiers jeered. And the man was gone, shoved before Simon and the cross, up the narrow street.

Mok stared at his fingertips, as if there might be a mark there. How could that slight touch have filled him with such utter serenity, such clear understanding of the love of the God of the universe?

It was such an incredible mixture of joy and peace that it took several minutes for Mok to comprehend something equally strange and unexpected and beautiful.

He no longer felt weak. The white heat of pain had disappeared. He no longer bled.

Mok had been healed.

With disbelief, he stared up the hill at the crowd that had left him behind.

But Mok did not want to be left behind. He began to run toward the man of the cross.

MOK COULD NOT FIGHT his way to the front of the procession. The crowd was too big, the street too narrow. He followed, all the while trying to make sense of his new surroundings.

He was in a city, of that he had no doubt. Every few paces, other streets led away from the one he walked. Crooked and twisting, they seemed to form a maze. Except for arched openings, the buildings of plastered white formed continuous lines so that the streets were almost like tunnels leading away in different directions. The people wore robes of all colors, many of the women with head coverings.

Jerusalem, Simon had said. *Jerusalem during Passover.*

It had been years since Mok had last held the audiobook of his childhood. Only fragments remained of what he could remember from that audiobook. Yet those fragments had sustained him during his years alone, struggling for survival in the desperate street slums of Old Newyork.

Jerusalem during Passover.

Mok's strongest impression of the audiobook had not been details, but hope. The legend of a man from Galilee, a man who had done wonderful things and helped many poor and lonely people, had given him hope. Mok wished he could be more certain of his memories, but hadn't the audiobook spoken of a place called Jerusalem?

As he wondered, the crowd spilled through a giant stone archway out of the city. With the buildings no longer surrounding him, Mok was able to see that they were among hills, which explained the angle of the streets. The land dropped steeply into a valley and rose just as steeply on the other side. He noticed the dusty green of stocky trees rising in small groves from the brown of arid land. Beyond, Mok saw the tops of other hills lined against the pale blue of the sky.

He did not spend much time surveying the view, for the crowd had spread, and he was able to push forward. It took him only minutes to reach the front.

What he saw shocked him. He briefly stepped backward in horror.

The cross that Simon had carried lay on the rocky ground. Simon was gone. The man of the cross, the man who had healed Mok, stood with his head bowed beside that cross. The Roman soldiers continued to guard him.

But this was not what horrified Mok. No, it was the sight of two more crosses, both of those also lying flat on the ground.

Nor was it simply those two crosses. Rather, it was the activity at each cross that shocked him.

For a man had been laid on each of those crosses. Those two men had been beaten, and soldiers held their arms along the beams of the crosses.

Mok had arrived at the very moment when a soldier had lifted a massive hammer and begun to pound an iron spike into the wood of the cross—through the hand of one of the men.

Thud. The hammer came down. Thud. Thud.

The man shrieked in agony. Half of the crowd roared approval while the other half wailed in protest. Unfazed by the reaction of the spectators, the soldier moved to the man's other hand and began the process again.

The second man, held by soldiers to the second cross on the ground, began to cry in fear. The third man, with the eyes of eternity, simply continued to stand quietly with his head bowed.

When the solider began to pound spikes into the ankles of the first man, Mok turned his head, unable to bear the sight of the blood. But the sounds still reached him.

Not once among all the cruelties that Mok had seen in the slums of Old Newyork had he ever seen anything close to this. He felt his stomach flipping, and Mok had to struggle to keep from vomiting.

It wasn't over.

The soldier with the hammer moved to the second man. Others lifted the first cross into place. On top of the hill, it stood outlined against the sky.

And other soldiers took the third man, the one who had healed Mok, and placed him on the third cross still on the ground. He did not protest. He did not cry out in fear. He quietly allowed the soldiers to stretch his arms into place.

"No!" The loud cry ripped itself from Mok, almost before he was aware he had joined the wailing of women nearby. "No!"

Mok knew nothing about why the men were being nailed to the beams of wood. He knew nothing about the men. Nothing except the depth of the third man's eyes and his gentleness and his promise to Mok just before their fingertips had brushed.

Even with what little he knew, Mok was as certain as he breathed that the third man did not deserve to be hung on a cross.

"No!" Mok cried. He rushed forward.

A soldier saw him and slammed his head with a sideways swing of his spear. Mok tumbled backward and lost all sight and sound to an overwhelming darkness. Not the familiar whirling darkness of cyberspace, but the painful darkness of losing consciousness.

CHAPTER 5

MOK WOKE to perfume. His head was cradled in a woman's lap. She gently wiped his face with a cool cloth.

"Who are you?" Mok asked.

"Mary Magdalene," she answered. "I have promised myself to care for you when I am able. But please forgive me. I cannot take you away from here yet."

Mok blinked. He saw he was still on the hillside. Surrounded by a crowd. All three crosses now stood against the sun.

The woman mistook his silence and hurried to explain more. "You tried to save our Teacher," she said. "You deserve help. But we cannot leave him."

She began to weep.

Mok ran his tongue over his teeth. None were broken. He eased up to a sitting position. His head throbbed, but aside from a tender spot where the spear had hit his skull, he felt no other damage.

The woman continued to weep. Another woman sat beside her and tried to comfort her.

"Mary, Mary," the other woman said, "remember his teachings. Remember his love."

"Who is that man?" Mok asked them both. "And why have they done this to him?"

Mary drew a deep breath. She straightened her posture. "He is Jesus of Nazareth. And the Romans have crucified him because—"

"Jesus of Nazareth!" Mok forgot his pain. "The Galilee Man!"

Mary nodded, puzzled at Mok's excitement. "Yes," she said with hesitation. "He is from Galilee."

Mok stared at the cross in awe. Jesus was not a legend, but truth! Mok had found the Galilee Man of his childhood audiobook!

In the same instant, Mok's joy turned to bitter sorrow. This Jesus was beaten and hanging from a cross—about to die. Where was the hope in that?

Unless the rest of the audiobook had also spoken the truth. Unless this Jesus would rise again from the dead as the audiobook had promised.

Mok marveled in silence. If the man named Jesus rose from the dead, he truly was the Son of the God of the universe. And if the Son of God had come to earth, how could any person knowing of it not choose to follow Jesus?

Yet . . .

Mok shook his head. Beaten and hanging from a cross. Could Mok really believe what seemed impossible, that this man would come to life again after death had taken him?

Mok wanted to believe. Mok also doubted.

He turned to Mary to ask her more questions.

But she was no longer there. Nor was the crowd. Nor anything else but the familiar darkness that told Mok he was about to be spun into a new time and place.

MAINSIDE. "Unbelievable!" the red-headed doctor said. "Cambridge. Look at this!"

Cambridge crossed the medical room in three quick, long steps. He stood beside the doctor at the cot where Mok lay motionless.

The doctor pointed at the various monitors of Mok's life-support system. "Everything is back to normal," the doctor said. "Pulse. Blood pressure. Even brain waves."

"Back to normal?" Cambridge asked.

"He was only moments away from death," the doctor said. "I can tell you in all my years as a doctor, I have never seen such a dramatic and complete recovery."

Cambridge bowed his head briefly. The doctor respected the silence. When Cambridge looked up again, the doctor continued.

"You and your prayers deserve full credit for whatever happened in cyberspace," the doctor said. "Nothing I did seemed to help."

Cambridge was about to reply, but he froze. And pointed.

On the cot, Mok opened his eyes.

CHAPTER 7

CAMBRIDGE'S OFFICE was the corner suite on the tenth floor of the luxury high-rise, down the hallway from where Mok had been. Floor to ceiling windows showed the Hudson River below, with the far shore-line that marked the island of Old Newyork. Ruins of the slum's skyscrapers, which had been scavenged for steel, rose against the bright sky beyond.

Cambridge pushed Mok's wheelchair to the window to let him stare out at the view. Cambridge moved to the corner of his desk and sat casually, half facing Mok, half toward the window.

Cambridge composed his thoughts. So much was happening so fast. Less than an hour earlier, Cambridge had confronted the Committee, about to reveal the traitor among them. Then the medical crisis with Mok had taken him away.

The Committee members were still under guard in the conference room, divided by the knowledge of a traitor among them, yet strangely united by their prayers for Mok. Cambridge had to deal with Mok before he returned to the Committee.

"You came from there," Cambridge finally said, pointing at the hazy, distant street canyons.

From his wheelchair, Mok squinted against the sunlight. It had taken half an hour to completely revive him. He had been motionless on the cot for so long that his muscles were still too weak to allow him to walk.

"Why should I believe you?" Mok asked after a long, thoughtful pause. "From what you said about this cyberspace . . ."

Cambridge hid a smile. In the half hour since Mok had returned, Cambridge had not had time to tell him much. An illiterate Welfaro would be expected to spend days trying to comprehend computers and cyberspace and virtual reality. Yet Mok had grasped the concept immediately.

"What I said about cyberspace was that the computer supplied your brain with the sights, smells, sounds, tastes, and touch of an artificial world. The program would adjust to the decisions you made, as you were making them. To your mind then—"

"I know, I know. To my mind then, the new worlds were completely real," Mok said. "Which is why I wonder if this, too, is part of cyberspace. You, too, could be part of the program. All of this could still be happening in my mind. It could simply be another cybersegment."

"It could," Cambridge finally allowed, impressed at Mok's logic. "Given the effectiveness of virtual reality, I'm not sure how I can convince you otherwise. Perhaps I can only ask you to listen as if you truly had returned."

Mok watched the distant skyline for five minutes.

Cambridge, acutely aware of the Committee crisis in the conference room, showed no signs of impatience. It was infinitely more important to convince Mok to join their cause.

"All right," Mok said, turning back to Cambridge. "It matters little to me how I was sent into those other worlds. I do, however, want to know why. If you promise to answer that, I will listen."

CHAPTER 8

"YOU WERE BORN into a world without hope," Cambridge began. "It is a giant prison where water is more precious than a person's blood. Books do not exist. Slaves work in factories for warlords. There are no hospitals or schools. No police."

Cambridge paused soberly. "Not that I need tell you this in great detail."

"No," Mok said quietly. A lifetime of memories of the harshness were enough reminder.

"Hopeless as it might seem," Cambridge continued, "I doubt those who live there would chose death over life."

"No," Mok said again, more quietly. He had seen how hard people fought to stay alive.

"Here on Mainside," Cambridge said, "the wealthy and powerful have determined that your life and those of others in Old Newyork are not worth sustaining. The World United government wishes to destroy Old Newyork. Most of the steel has been scavenged. They see no reason to continue supplying water. At the end of the month, they intend to . . ."

Cambridge stared away from Mok, at the slums. Lost in contemplation of the horror.

"Yes?" Mok prompted.

"Heat bombs. Far, far more effective than the atomic bombs of another age. The concrete and glass of the entire island will fuse. No man, woman, or child will survive."

"What?!" Mok half stood, then grunted in pain and fell back in his wheelchair.

Cambridge got up from his desk and began pacing the office as he spoke. "You asked me why you were sent into cyberspace. Let me answer by telling you about a man named Benjamin Rufus. Decades ago, he founded the Benjamin Rufus Corporation, a giant Internet company, and became one of the wealthiest men on the planet. Twenty years ago, he gave up wealth, power, everything to go from Mainside into Old Newyork. Why? He wanted to begin change there."

"He could have sent someone else," Mok said.

"Perhaps. But he had reasons to go himself. On Mainside he left behind his corporation, its money, and a committee of men directed to use the profits to accomplish what Rufus planned to begin himself in Old Newyork before he died. He wanted to establish a better life for the people in Old Newyork. Especially for its children.

"There are hundreds of thousands in the slums," Cambridge said. "It seemed an impossible task, with the ganglords and the slave factories and the total chaos of a giant prison without laws. But Rufus began an underground church in Old

Newyork, bringing the message of eternal hope to a place where the gospel of Jesus Christ had been lost over the generations."

"The Galilee Man!" Mok said.

Cambridge smiled. "Yes, Jesus of Nazareth. Yet mere words of hope were not enough. In the slums, we continued Rufus's mission by developing hidden pockets of Christians who helped others. Not Churchians, who simply preached and judged those who would not follow their rules, but followers of Jesus, who acted, mostly in secret, to help others."

Mok smiled. "Now I understand the stories. Time and again in the slums, I heard about women and children who were rescued or given food but didn't know who to thank for the help."

"Yes," Cambridge said. "It was not yet time for them to move openly. Even then, these small groups who lead by example were able to bring others to follow the Galilee Man. Hundreds of groups formed over the years, but no group included more than a dozen people.

"Because of the thousands and thousands in the slums and the threat of ganglords, we needed to maintain secrecy until we were ready. Our final goal was to send a single leader into the slums, a leader who could use the full wealth and power of the Benjamin Rufus corporation to unite these underground Christians in an open struggle against the evil in the slums."

Cambridge stopped pacing. He stood beside Mok's wheelchair.

"We had set up the cybertests to find a leader to send into Old Newyork to unite the underground movement," Cambridge said. "This leader has to be strong, trustworthy. For this leader, once free in the slums with the money and help from us on Mainside, would literally have the unchecked power of a king."

Cambridge put his hand on Mok's shoulder. "Remember Egypt? We need someone who has a sense of justice so strong that he would face death rather than let another die for him. The castle? We need someone willing to stand firm in his faith, no matter how great the pressure to do otherwise. And so on. Each stage was a way to test our candidate. A dozen of the best-educated Mainsiders failed. We had no leader. Until you."

"Me?"

"Only you passed, Mok. Only you made it through all the cybertests. My great regret is that you were sent into the test without your permission. You were the only candidate who didn't realize he *was* a candidate. Almost the way a baby is born and must live through the quest of life."

"I would have accepted the challenge had you asked," Mok said.

"That pleases me," Cambridge said. "Yet with all the choices you made in all those times and places, there remains another. Will you accept the leadership? Because now, even that slight hope for Old Newyork is in danger."

Cambridge shook his head sadly. "I told you of the government proposal to simply erase Old Newyork. Certain real estate developers can't wait to get their hands on the land. The bill has been drafted. Tomorrow, it goes to a final vote. Our sources tell us that of the fifteen hundred senators, seven hundred will vote in favor of dropping the heat bombs, seven hundred will vote against, and one hundred are undecided."

"What can I do?" Mok asked.

"Stand up before the World Senate. Help us convince fifty-one out of those final one hundred not to vote for the total destruction of Old Newyork."

Mok frowned. "They have no reason to listen to me."

Cambridge allowed himself a mysterious smile. "I believe they do. Please remember two things about what I'm going to tell you next. First, it must remain a sworn secret between us until the time is right."

"And second?" Mok asked.

"What I have to tell you will make your decision to help us much more difficult than you can imagine."

CHAPTER 9

ONE HOUR LATER, Cambridge and Mok stood at the head of a long table in the conference room. Behind them was a large, gray screen—the screen that had allowed the Committee to view Mok's cyberadventures.

The Committee members waited for Cambridge to speak. Cambridge gestured at the coffee cups and plates of half-eaten food scattered around the table.

"You have waited with great patience," Cambridge said. "I believe you will have found it worth your while."

Cambridge smiled. "Let me introduce Mok. You've shared his cyberadventures. You've been grateful for his decisions. And now, by a miracle, he is with us after the World War II shooting. I'm pleased to say he has accepted our request to return to Old Newyork."

When the applause died down, Cambridge looked at his watch.

"Some of you may find it hard to believe that only half the morning has passed since you gathered for our emergency meeting," Cambridge said. "I regret the guards in the hallway, but as you know, one of us has betrayed the cause. Were it not for Mok's medical crisis . . ."

Many of the Committee nodded. All of them understood.

"Anyway," Cambridge said, "it is time to finish the difficult task that began this morning."

Cambridge turned to Mok. "You should know what has happened. While you were in cyberspace, a killer was sent after you."

"Barbarossa," Mok whispered. "On the pirate ship."

Cambridge nodded. "And in real time, another killer made an attempt—here in this building. That assassin was caught. Plastic surgery had made him identical in appearance to Committee member Stimpson."

All eyes turned to Stimpson. He sat at the far end of the table, a blue-eyed man with blond hair carefully brushed back in the latest Technocrat style. His teeth—capped, of course—were shiny white and perfect. His nose was straight, his cheek-bones high as current fashion dictated. Most Technocrats had plastic surgery at least once every ten years, and Stimpson's appearance showed the results of such care and attention.

"It was a stroke of genius on the part of whoever paid the assassin," Cambridge said. "Our surveillance cameras clearly showed the killer's face. Had he escaped, we would have all believed he was Stimpson, not an impersonator."

Murmurs of sympathy spread around the table for Stimpson.

"Yet," Cambridge said to Mok, "we did find a way to trap the Committee member who was responsible for betraying the sequence code that allowed the killer Barbarossa into cyberspace after you. This occurred during your time in the cybersegment set in France."

Cambridge then turned to the others. "I won't drag this out farther. This morning, all of you heard the details of how we set up ghost sites in cyberspace to monitor your activities. When one of you made a move against Mok, we knew exactly which one of you is the betrayer."

Cambridge pointed at a man sitting on the left-hand side of the table. He was a dark-haired man of medium height and medium build.

"It is you, Phillips," Cambridge said. "This Committee has been dedicated to its cause for twenty years. All this time you have worked with us, eaten with us, shared with us. There should be no punishment too great for one who betrays friends. However, that is not for us to decide. Harming you will harm your family, and they do not deserve to share in your punishment. Instead, we will send you away, trusting that God's judgment will be rendered when he sees fit."

Phillips bowed his head as shouts of anger echoed through the room. Several men leaned across the table, as if to grab him.

"No!" Cambridge ordered. "We will not add a crime of revenge to his crime of betrayal."

In the following stunned silence, Cambridge turned to Phillips. "Have you anything to say?"

Phillips shook his head.

"Then go," Cambridge said. "We have greater concerns than your miserable existence."

Phillips pushed his chair away from the table. Silently, he walked from the room. Not one Committee member turned to watch his departure.

CHAPTER 10

IN THE MORNING SUNSHINE, Cambridge and Mok stood at the bottom of the wide marble steps of the Great Congress Hall of the World United government. Hundreds of men and women of all nations filled the steps, talking to each other in groups of twos and threes and fours.

Mok looked younger than he had the day before. A blue silk toga had transformed him from a slum dweller to a handsome young Technocrat.

Mok scanned the scene, intent on observing as much as he could. This site and these politicians, Cambridge had explained, ruled the destiny of the world's billions of people.

The building before him reflected that importance. It seemed to reach as high as a mountain, with huge columns of polished stone supporting the arched marble of the entrances.

A bell began to ring, chiming three times and pausing before ringing three more times. Again and again. People began to flow up toward the main entrance.

"It is time," Cambridge said. "Everything depends on the next few hours."

The ceiling of the hall was a large graceful curve at least three stories above the assembled senators. It reflected sound so clearly that the speaker at the front of the giant hall did not need a microphone to address the 1,500 people assembled.

He raised his hands and received instant silence, the traditional respect given to the president of the World United. Mok and Cambridge, sitting in guest seats near the back, heard clearly, for the interior was built for the slightest sounds to travel without echoing.

"As you all know by your agenda," the president said, "we will begin by reviewing the status of the slum area known as Old Newyork."

Behind him were three vidscreens, each two stories tall. While the outside screens were blank, the middle screen showed the speaker himself. His black silk toga hung from a tall and bulky body. He had white hair that made a sharp contrast with pale skin, flushed slightly pink. His voice was deep and commanding. Even without the presidency to cloak him with power, he was an intimidating man.

"Administration staff has reviewed all the debate requests and narrowed them down to two," the president continued. "As usual, each side will be represented once, with time allotted for counterpoints. I trust you have all read the overview for finer details."

Cambridge leaned over to whisper to Mok. "With so many bills in each session," he explained, "senators rarely take time to read the reports. That's why what we say will be so important."

Mok nodded and swallowed, trying to work moisture into a mouth dry from nervousness.

"I now invite the Honorable Senator from Jersey North to come forward."

Cambridge whispered again as they watched a short, bald man walk with a cane toward the podium.

"Look to the right of the screens," Cambridge said. "You see that large black square with hundreds of small lights?"

"Yes," Mok whispered in return. Some were lit red, some green, and some white.

"A hundred years ago, before the World United assumed its role as the seat of world power, voting was done differently. Senators listened to endless arguments and only voted once. Now debate is limited by a preset time, and senators vote by pushing one of three buttons before them. They are free to change their votes as often as they want until time has run out. The count that stands then is considered the final vote. It has become something like the running scoreboard of a sporting match, and debaters play their arguments accordingly. You'll see that the board already shows some totals."

Mok gave no comment about the numbers on the board.

"I'm sorry," Cambridge said. "I forget you are handicapped by a lack of formal education. Don't be embarrassed that you cannot read. I'll simply explain."

The bald senator with a cane had almost reached the podium.

"The totals at this point reflect what we expected," Cambridge whispered. "There are seven hundred and three red lights, showing votes in favor of destroying Old Newyork, and seven hundred and two green lights against. The ninety-five white lights indicate the undecided senators."

The giant middle screen showed the senator's round-faced image, magnifying large eyebrows that seemed to hold all the hair missing from his scalp.

"Honorable Senators," he began, "my argument will be brief, simply because not much needs to be said. For decades, we have funneled criminals into Old Newyork. We send millions of gallons of pure water into the slums and in return receive less and less steel each day. Should we continue to take water away from our children and our law-abiding citizens? Should we continue to support lawless scum who murder each other and force the weak among them to work as slaves? The answer is no.

"Think of this as a war for survival, not unlike the great Water Wars. In each of your countries, millions died then. Should we let those millions of deaths mean nothing against the relatively few people in Old Newyork who take such a large amount of water? Should we give away water that was bought by the blood of your own people?"

The senator paused dramatically and spoke quietly, which made the entire audience lean forward. "In Old Newyork, they are not people but lawless animals. Erase them now and your voters will thank you by returning you to office next election."

He paused again. "Remember, it is not about what you feel, but about what your voters want. And you know voters care far more for their own water than for the scum who fill that island prison. So, ask yourself, do you each want to remain a World United senator?"

He stepped away from the podium and leaned on his cane as he hobbled back toward his seat. His slow, painful progress down the long aisle presented the picture of a noble man suffering for a righteous cause.

At first slowly, and then as fast as blinking eyes, green lights began to change to red. Before the senator had reached his seat again, the totals showed 53 undecided and 466 against. Nine hundred and eighty-one votes now favored total destruction of Old Newyork.

CHAPTER 11

THE PRESIDENT RETURNED to the podium. He consulted his notes. The giant screen showed that he held every muscle on his face motionless as he called for the next speaker.

"Countering the words of our Honorable Senator from Jersey North," the president said, "will be a common citizen named Johnson Cambridge."

Murmurs rose among the senators.

"Silence in the Assembly," the president ordered. "While this is unusual, Cambridge is speaking on behalf of African Senator Harper Chaim."

The president cleared his throat. The giant screen made it obvious that he was furrowing his eyebrows in disapproval. "I want the Assembly to note that Cambridge is from the Benjamin Rufus Corporation, one of the world's largest single companies. I also think it fair to note that the Rufus Corporation donates millions of dollars each year to Senator Chaim's region. You are thus forewarned of the obvious monetary reason for Senator Chaim to step aside, and you are welcome to vote accordingly."

Immediately, more of the green and white lights flicked to red.

As Cambridge and Mok stood, a ripple of boos greeted them. Cambridge spoke quietly to Mok as they walked the aisle to the podium. "That was an unfair introduction. Those millions are spent in helping Chaim's people develop farmland to feed themselves."

Mok was concentrating too hard on walking straight ahead to reply. He was afraid of tripping with all the eyes upon him.

Finally they reached the podium and, side by side, faced the entire Assembly. Cambridge was forced to wait until the scattered booing ended.

"If your argument is water," Cambridge said, "Old Newyork will *give* you water."

He braced himself on the podium with both hands and leaned forward. "Yes. You heard me correctly. Old Newyork will not take millions of gallons of water from Mainside; it will produce not only enough water for itself but also extra water to be shipped into Mainside."

Senators began flipping through the pages in their reports. This was an incredible piece of news.

"You will not find that proposal in your notes," Cambridge said. "It was not until yesterday that the owner of the Benjamin Rufus Corporation signed an agreement to invest twenty billion dollars in large-scale water purification factories to be constructed in Old Newyork. These water converters—

not steel scavenging, not slave factories—will be the basis of Old Newyork's new economy."

Red lights began to turn green. Within seconds, nearly the entire board glowed green.

The president strode forward and held up his hands for silence.

"Assembly," the president said, "that I am using my position to break into this debate shows the seriousness of my concerns. Some of you are swayed too easily by promises. I will pose questions of hard reality for our visitor. How do you expect to convince Mainside workers to enter the slum prison of Old Newyork? And once there, how would you expect to protect them against the ganglords who run the slave factories?"

Cambridge smiled a peaceful smile. "Your Worldship, it will be people within Old Newyork who work at the water purification converters. Not Mainsiders."

The president laughed. "Those people have no education. No law. They are animals that cannot be tamed, no matter how many soldiers you might send into the slums."

Green lights began turning back to red.

Cambridge's peaceful smile did not waver. "Your Worldship, I agree this is a bold plan. I believe that within a year, the people themselves will provide their own law and order, their own schooling."

The president snorted. "How do you expect this insane plan to work?"

"Christian principles," Cambridge said. "As simple as it seems, people in Old Newyork will help one another, following in the footsteps of Jesus Christ of Nazareth."

"Christianity is outlawed!" the president said in a half-shout.

"With all due respect, Your Worldship, as you have pointed out, there are no laws in Old Newyork. There, then, the Mainside ban against Christianity does not apply."

More than a few faces in the large crowd grinned with appreciation at the truth in Cambridge's loophole. Yet no more of the lights changed to green; all attention was on the debate, not the voting.

Cambridge turned to appeal to the senators. "The Benjamin Rufus Corporation has found some-one who will unite an existing underground move-ment in the slums. This person will be granted the resources of the Benjamin Rufus Corporation to deliver food, teachers, police, and whatever else is required to give the people of the slums a chance to save themselves."

Cambridge pointed to the giant screen on his left. "In moments, you will see that person. You will see scenes from cyberspace that tested him to the utmost. All I ask is that you watch and make your decision accordingly. Yes, I know you will have many questions about the details of the Rufus Corporation plan. These will be answered in a full report to your administration. For now, honorable senators, all we ask is that you vote to delay the destruction of Old Newyork for two years. Give us that chance."

Cambridge nodded at a comtech. Seconds later, images began appearing on the screen. First came an animated explanation of how cyberspace worked, how the candidate did not know he had been placed in cyberspace, and the purpose of each of the cybertests. Then, in full color, Mok saw the actions that were stamped in his memory as surely as if they had been real.

He watched the crucial moments of his time in ancient Egypt, with execution a threat. The Holy Land castle. The pirate ship. The Wild West. France and World War II in 1943.

Mok squirmed with embarrassment at all the attention. Yet when the cybersegments ended, many of the senators rose and applauded him.

In the silence that followed, Cambridge spoke again, more quietly.

"This young man before you is the same candidate you saw on the screen. His name is Mok, and he is from Old Newyork. He survived a quest that has prepared him to return to the slums and help his people, fully backed by the world's largest corporation. How then do you vote?"

Nearly all the red lights and nearly all the white lights disappeared in a blur of green.

"No!" It was the president's turn to speak. "Let the Assembly know that this man is lying. Think! The Benjamin Rufus Corporation is famous because its founder did not leave an heir. Have you forgotten it is run by a Board of Directors? When Cambridge said the owner has agreed to invest billions in Old Newyork, he was telling you something impossible. And if that is impossible, we cannot believe the corporation is willing to put its resources into helping the people of the slums."

Lights began to flick back to red.

Cambridge nodded at Mok.

Mok put up his hand with some uncertainty. His movement directed the president's attention to him.

"Yes?" the president asked with a snarl.

Mok stepped directly behind the podium. "Honorable senators," Mok began. His voice croaked. He licked his lips and tried again. "Honorable senators, Cambridge did not lie. Yesterday, the owner of the Benjamin Rufus Corporation did review plans for water purification. Yesterday, the owner did approve those plans."

Mok took a deep breath. "How do I know?"

He took another deep breath to speak. "I am that owner. I am the son of Benjamin Rufus. I have inherited his corporation."

"NO! NO! NO!" the president thundered.

Hundreds of excited small discussions stopped among the senators. The president pointed at the vote board, lit with 1,328 green lights.

"Five minutes remain until the vote is frozen," said the president, slightly calmer. "By then, I expect a majority vote in favor of destroying Old Newyork."

If possible, the Assembly grew even quieter.

"As you know, the office of president allows for an override of majority if the president deems this an issue of global security," he continued. "I have received reports that the ganglords intend to break out of Old Newyork and begin war on Mainsiders. It is not something I wanted made public for fear of starting a panic. This, however, leaves me no choice. I command you to vote for the destruction of Old Newyork."

He, and his large image on the screen, glared out at the Assembly.

Slowly, the green lights began to switch to red. Within a minute, the vote board was as red as it had been green earlier.

"Thank you," the president said. He looked at the clock. "Soon the vote will be official. After tomorrow, Old Newyork will exist no more. Now we can move onto less troublesome Assembly matters."

The president turned to Cambridge and Mok. "You are invited to leave."

"No," Cambridge said boldly for all the senators to hear. "You have lied. There is no plan for ganglords to break out."

"How dare you accuse me of lying?! What would I have to gain by that?! Guards—"

Without warning, the live image of the president wavered on the large center screen. It went blank. A new vidsegment appeared, showing two men on a bench in a park. As the camera closed in on the two men, audio broke through, interrupting the president's command. When the recorded voices echoed through the hall, the president snapped around to see what was happening on the screen.

It was his voice that reached the senators, his face clear on the giant screen.

"You want payment?" the president was saying to the other man. "Don't be ridiculous. Our deal was simple. Find a way to kill that miserable slum kid before he passed all their cybertests. But Mok is not dead. He is due to testify tomorrow before the Assembly of Senators. I will not pay you a thing."

"Yes, you will, Your Worldship." The camera closed in on the other man. Not Phillips, as Mok had expected, but the Committee member named Stimpson. *Stimpson?* Mok wanted to turn to

Cambridge and ask about this unexpected sight, but Stimpson continued to speak and Mok didn't want to miss a word. "I have recorded many of our conversations. If you don't pay, I'll go public."

The president at the podium shouted at the comtechs. "Stop! Stop!"

The comtechs lifted their hands in bewilderment, as if they, too, were unable to understand how this vidsegment was overriding their controls.

The president ran to the screen. He tried to pull it down. It was a futile attempt, for the screen towered over him like a building.

"Blackmail?" the image of the president snorted on the vidscreen. "You fool. The men who have arranged to buy the land base of Old Newyork once it's destroyed are men with enormous power. Even I am afraid of what they might do to me if I do not get the World Senate to vote for the heat bombs. If you attempt to blackmail me, you will be dead within days, no matter where you try to hide."

On the vidscreen, the president rose from the park bench. "However, it will be less troublesome to throw you a bone than to risk inquiries that might result from your death. I will make billions for my part in this, and I am willing to toss you a few million. Send me all the recorded conversations, and my secretary will credit whatever bank account you prefer. Remember, though, if you ever attempt to blackmail me or even contact me again, you will be killed."

The screen went blank.

The president turned from his vain efforts to pull down the screen. He faced the Assembly.

As one person, all the senators rose and began to boo.

The president fell to his knees.

Mok raised his voice to be heard as he spoke to Cambridge. "The other man on the Committee? Phillips? He was not the traitor?"

"Phillips agreed to take the blame," Cambridge said. "So that we could follow the real betrayer. Stimpson. It was brilliant on his part to arrange the plastic surgery for the assassin to look like him. We would have never suspected him without the ghost-site trap that gave him away."

"But in the meeting—" Mok began.

"We wanted Stimpson to feel safe enough to approach whoever had paid him to betray us," Cambridge explained. "Field ops followed him with long-range vidcams. We never dreamed we'd get a segment as good as we did. From there, it was simple to plug the vidsegment into the programming here."

The booing continued. But the senators were doing one other thing. Still standing, they reached down to their vote buttons.

For the final time, red lights began to change to green. When the time limit ended, not one light on the vote board showed red or white.

CHAPTER 13

A SMALL BREEZE riffled the Hudson River below an overcast sky. Cambridge and Mok stood at the rails of a ferry, staring across at the skyline of Old Newyork.

"You know, of course, that a few years ago the Committee completed a tunnel beneath the river," Cambridge said.

"Over the years, that is how you have helped build the underground churches that wait for our arrival," Mok replied.

"You listen well. So now you might wonder why we are on this ferry instead."

Metal gates clanked behind them as the ferry left the dock.

"Sentimental reasons," Cambridge continued. "It was on a ferry like this that I last saw your father, some twenty years ago. He was doing much as you are, leaving behind the power and wealth of the Benjamin Rufus Corporation to help those in Old Newyork. It just seems right that you also return by ferry."

"I wish I could remember him," Mok said. "And I wish I could remember my mother."

"I understand," Cambridge answered quietly. The ferry pushed against the river current. It was only a ten-minute ride, but the shores of each side were worlds apart. "All I can tell you about your mother is what I learned from Benjamin."

Cambridge paused. The ferry engines hummed in the background.

"Your father went into Old Newyork with a lung disease, only expecting to live for a few months," Cambridge explained. "He had a vidphone of course, which is how I stayed in contact with him. When your mother helped him escape from a ganglord named Zubluk, they spent enough time together to fall in love. I believe it was their love that kept him alive for two more years."

Cambridge paused.

"He was there to bring the New Testament news . . ." Mok said, to encourage his friend to keep speaking.

"Yes. Imagine a generation of people cut off from any books or news. Benjamin wanted to give them hope, much as Jesus has done for people of all centuries. As long as he had strength to continue, we arranged for people being exiled to Old Newyork to smuggle audiobooks and other supplies to help him begin underground churches.

"For two years, he avoided Zubluk and the other ganglords. When it looked like the disease was certain to take him, he found a way to end the fight. With Zubluk gone, you and your mother were safe.

The other ganglords battled each other to take Zubluk's territory. The confusion gave the Christian followers a much better chance of growing."

Cambridge turned to Mok and smiled. "Of course, Benjamin Rufus left behind more than that. You."

Mok nodded, feeling a mixture of sadness and joy.

"I'm not sure when or how your mother died," Cambridge said. "But I do know that she left you an audiobook so that you could learn without her. As for your father, he left—"

"One of the world's largest corporations," Mok said.

"More than that, Mok." Cambridge's smile turned the older man's face from intense to peaceful. "A tiny transmitter, implanted in the skin just below your ankle. He had a plan for you from the very beginning."

Mok raised his eyebrows.

"It was difficult for me," Cambridge said. "Many nights I laid awake wondering if I should take you from the slums and put you in your rightful place here on Mainside. But already the Committee was looking for a way to find a leader . . ."

"All along you knew where I was?" Mok asked.

"You were lonely," Cambridge said. "But not alone. Field ops watched over you all through your childhood. Several times, we had members of the underground churches try to talk to you, but you always ran away."

"I trusted no one in the slums," Mok said. "It

seemed the only way to survive."

"Many were the times I wondered if we should just bring you to Mainside instead of leaving you alone in the slums," Cambridge said. "I regret I couldn't have made your childhood better."

Mok thought about it. "You shouldn't have. Remember, you said my quest was as a baby is born into life—with no choice but to go forward. It was the same way then in Old Newyork. All of us live the same way. Lonely but not alone. God was with me, and the home he promises is much greater than a corporation waiting on Mainside."

"Yes," Cambridge said simply. "Thank you."

They let some silence pass. The ferry was halfway across the river.

"There is something else you should know," Cambridge said, so quiet that Mok barely heard him above the splash of water against the ferry's hull. "You may hear of it in Old Newyork, and I want you to be prepared. It's about Benjamin Rufus."

"Tell me," Mok said.

"As a young man, he was sent to Old Newyork as a prisoner, for fraud. It was his idea to convert the slum dwellers into factory slaves. It was how he began his fortune, how he was able to raise enough money to bribe his way back to Mainside. Finally, after discovering wealth and power did not bring peace, he looked for the answers to life. And he began to follow Jesus, the Galilee Man. That was why he dedicated everything he had to bringing hope back to the slums. Now you can finish undoing his great wrong."

Mok would have replied, except an approaching passenger caught his eye. The sight stunned him.

"Voice-in-the-Wind," he whispered, more to himself than to Cambridge.

For it was. The pharaoh's daughter. The servant girl in the castle. The beautiful Pawnee of the western plains. Slim and tall with long dark hair, she walked closer and closer, smiling at Mok.

Cambridge saw Mok's attention was elsewhere and turned to see.

"Oh," Cambridge said. "Mok, let me introduce you to Madeline. She and I were your cyberguides."

"She?" Mok sputtered. Cyberguides. They had shown up at different times in different places, telling him just enough to help, but not enough to let him know what was happening. *These two were the cyberguides?* "You?"

"As I recall," Cambridge said, "it was in ancient Egypt that you first insisted on the name Stinko for me."

"You? The dwarf?"

"It was one of the more fun aspects of your quests," Cambridge said. "Madeline and I got hooked up to other computers and traveled through cyberspace to deliver messages to you."

Mok just shook his head.

"Anyway," Cambridge went on. "Madeline will be helping us over the next years in Old Newyork. You may not have realized it, but this is our chance to prove that faith can change lives. If we can show the world what faith can do, I'm certain the day will come when Christianity will not be outlawed on Mainside."

"She . . . is . . . helping . . ." Mok had trouble speaking.

"Don't be so surprised," Cambridge said. "Madeline is my daughter."

She smiled at Mok. He wanted to be angry for how she had tormented him in cyberspace, but all he could think of was the time they had ahead—and that mysterious smile of hers.

The ferry changed course as it made final adjustments to connect with the farside dock, now only a hundred yards away.

"Nearly there, Mok," Cambridge said. "This is your last chance. If you stay on the ferry, you can return to Mainside and a corporation worth billions."

"No," Mok said firmly. "I saw Jesus allow soldiers to nail spikes into his flesh. Whatever sacrifice I make is nothing compared to that."

Cambridge clutched Mok's shoulders. "What? You saw soldiers nail . . ."

"At the cross. In cyberspace. You know, when you sent me to Jerusalem for Jesus to heal my gunshot wound."

Mok could not understand why Cambridge looked so surprised.

It took until the ferry banged against the dock for Cambridge to be able to reply.

"Mok," Cambridge said, his voice shaky, "some will say it was your own memory, reaching for fragments from the audiobook of your childhood. Others will say it truly was a miracle, that Jesus did reach out and touch you in your moment of greatest need."

"What are you trying to tell me?" Mok asked.

"After you were shot in the cybersegment in Paris, we lost all cybercontact with you. We were certain you would die."

Comprehension and awed wonder flashed across Mok's face.

"Yes," Cambridge said with equal awe. "We did not program a cybersegment to put you at the cross of Jesus. Whatever happened there, happened without us."

Now Mok knew for certain. The man on the cross still lived.

AUTHOR NOTE

Mok's story is actually two stories. One of the stories is described in this cyberepisode.

There is also a series story linking together all the CyberQuest *books—the reason Mok has been sent into cyberspace. That story starts in* Pharaoh's Tomb *(#1) and is completed in* Galilee Man *(#6). No matter where you start reading Mok's story, you can easily go back to any book in the series without feeling like you already know too much about how the series story will end.*

This series story takes place about a hundred years in the future. You will see that parts of Mok's world are dark and grim. Yet, in the end, this is a story of hope, the most important hope any of us can have. We, too, live in a world that at times can be dark and grim. During his cyberquest, Mok will see how Jesus Christ and his followers have made a difference over the ages.

Some of you may be reading this series after following Mok's adventures in Breakaway, *a* Focus on the Family *magazine for teen guys. Those magazine episodes were the inspiration for the* CyberQuest *series, and I would like to* thank Michael Ross and Jesse Flores at Breakaway for all the fun we had working together. However, this series contains far more than the original stories—once I really started to explore Mok's world, it became obvious to me that there was too much of the story left to be told. So, if you're joining this adventure because of Breakaway, I think I can still promise you plenty of surprises.

Last, thank you for sharing Mok's world with me. You are the ones who truly bring Mok and his friends and enemies to life.

From your friend,

Sigmund Brouwer